THE DAMAGE WE DO

DAVID ROSE

THE DAMAGE WE DO © 2025 David Rose

Published by Graveside Press
graveside-press.com

Editing: Kelley York
Proofreading: Syd Tomac
Cover illustration: IlluMax Illustration and Design
Cover typography and layout: Sleepy Fox Studio
Interior Formatting: Sleepy Fox Studio

Digital 978-1-967547-55-5
Paperback (Trade) 978-1-967547-54-8

GRAVESIDE·PRESS

Content Notes

For a list of potentially triggering content, please skip to page 70.

DAY ONE

I

THE JOLTING FOUR-BY-FOUR PUNCHES me repeatedly in my sensitive, metallic ovaries. The remnant of my period is shuffling its zombie gait into my lower abdomen. It is on the left side this month. That, the car sickness, and the wish not to be touched by Daan, all rise like a worn nausea. His hand feigns affection by falling on my knee. I swat it away. It falls pointlessly on the automatic gear stick, pretending it has something to do there. The same thing it would have done on my knee.

"They wrote to say it would be a bumpy ride," Daan says, and I recognise the tone. The voice to coax my anger away, to placate the rising fury he no doubt sees on my face. It won't work. It just winds my springs more. Those rusty, creaking springs, nestled deep inside which tighten every month and spit out excess.

"Looks like good hiking country. We can all go tomorrow, pop Evi into the papoose. I'll carry Luuk when he needs It."

I don't want to hike. I don't even want to be here. But he'll plead, beg, then insist, threaten. I will have to agree. I shall fake illness. Again. He glances over and sees the discomfort on my face. When I don't respond, he adds: "Only three more kilometres like this."

Only three more kilometres, after the other two thousand from Rotterdam, playing "Ik zie ik zie wat jij niet ziet" with Luuk and feeding Evi in motorway stations. Feeding her homogenised chemicals in small jars because she no longer wants my milk. She never wanted it.

"Are we there yet?" screams Luuk from the back seat. "Are we there yet?"

And repeat.

The —no, *directly*—Evi's fault. There was me with my distorted, bumpy body that was once slender, pumping out milk, a factory on legs, to the rhythm of my tears and her cries. My tears washed away by the vicious, flagellating water drops as I sobbed in the shower. Crying aloud without reserve, *"She no longer wants my milk,"* knowing the words were nothing but hormones, chemical messages in informational packets of passions.

I could hear Daan popping open another jar in the front room before he ascended the narrow stairs with his supposed solution. "Let's go away. Get in the car and just drive."

Daan and Evi no longer have a purpose for me. And, like he did with Luuk, he will take over. I only serve one purpose for Daan, to relieve his stress, to be there for him. To listen and never to question. To flinch.

And drive we did. Through Luuk's persistent and inane questions, through his loud tantrums, through Germany, through Daan's understated misery and my silent, silent gaze. Through Austria, through Evi's incessant screaming. Through Croatia and a thousand hopes dashed like flies on the windscreen. Then, through the land where Roman letters fall away to be replaced by unintelligible squiggles. And all the way through nausea, through shitty nappies and regurgitated food, through that egoistic bike waiting to be ridden "for once not on the flat of the low countries" with a smile and a nudge and hearing me all alone, with a crying, rejecting, resentful baby who hates me for bringing her to light and whom I cannot love and a small dwarf who looks on me like an alien waiting for his father to finish filling the petrol and come back and not to leave him alone with me. And me, who sees them as other, as not mine, as *wanting* to love, thinking I *ought* to love, but made to do it through expectation. I'm weeping again. Daan looks with too much concentration into his side mirror.

We arrive at a gate. It says, in English, "Horses Only." In German, someone has added, "But horses can't read."

"That's the one," says Daan, jumping too eagerly from the car. I watch him open the gate, climb back behind the wheel, drive through, jump out and close it. The ferrous smell of damp earth pollutes the car. Luuk sniffs loudly. I almost snap, as though he should control himself.

Evi is crying. Always crying. I wonder why Luuk doesn't ask me why. I turn and shout at Evi. It does no good. Luuk's lip trembles and he quickly looks out of the window, his eyes moist.

I want to say sorry. I want to cry. A pain sears into my left side and I gulp down some vomit.

Daan bounces back in. Tigger on E. His forced happiness squeezes the air of the car out. "Off we go," he says cheerily, ignoring the tear on the cheek of his child. Like a middle-aged scout master whose wife is having an affair.

I think about an impenetrable alleyway between the car seats, between Luuk and Evi, me and myself. I fucking hate Daan. I place my hand on his knee and smile. He finds a smile of his own from somewhere. It's difficult for him to meet my gaze.

II

Does he want me to make the decision? This was all his fucking idea, anyway. Why should I have to figure this out? Why me?

"You're so indecisive," I state as a matter of fact. He does his best spaniel impression.

"It's late," he says.

So? I think. But I repeat, "Yes, late."

We're all talking over each other in English. The owner, twice my husband's age, explaining the problem with the room booking, his wordless wife, seemingly even older, and us two. Daan's is comical, as always. He has that Dutch vice of sounding like a lisping vacuum cleaner at times. I wait for him to make mistakes and then correct him. He laughs but his eyes are angry.

The Swedish woman's, Ebba's, is as good as mine when she does speak. Her eyes are solitary. I recognise that. As my husband looks at his phone, our gazes meet; we see each other's loneliness.

"Are you alone?" I ask. "It seems lonely here."

Daan lumbers around, trying to find a signal. "I have one bar," he shouts triumphantly. My phone has nothing. No chance to book a hotel in a city online. We are stuck.

Ebba flinches as a tall man, all wrinkles and tired skin, joins her, shrinking her even more. A broken doll turned in on itself and slightly worn. He wraps an arm around her like a skeletal branch, and with the other—long and spindly—takes Daan's hand. He squeezes.

"Hi, I'm Brad." An American, the twang is redneck from a thousand Hollywood films. He smiles at me, all pointy teeth and possession. "Welcome to Bathory House. Happy to have you here."

I doubt they are. We pay, that is all.

Brad turns to Luuk, towering over him. He towers over Daan and me, too, which is uncomfortable for a Dutch couple. We're used to being the tallest in the room. But, his tall is the wrong sort. All lithe, forced, bones stretched and ironed into new combinations. More elbows and knees than he should have.

"You've got to hold and squeeze. Look me right in the eyes," he tells my four-year-old son.

Fucking hell. He's one of *those*. A man's man. Open car doors, walk near the road, slap them when they're mouthy. I've lived with one. Daan is different. Not better, *different*.

Luuk has not yet been corrupted.

"He's just a boy," I interject.

"In the eyes," he repeats to Luuk's downcast, timid head. Those irises are blue. Deep, but watery, blue. They stretch back to a past.

Luuk is trying to look him in the eyes now. His own are welling up. *Get away from my fucking son,* my ovaries scream. Evi cries out and Brad is distracted.

"I'm Mila," I tell him, breaking his focus. "That's Evi. Do you want to squeeze her hand, too?"

Silence from Brad. Silence from Daan. Then Brad laughs. Too long. Too loud. *Back the fuck off,* I think, and say it with my face.

Ebba mumbles something. Her voice has gone quieter in his presence. She is shrunken, tiny, made of porcelain. I feel no sympathy for her, only fear. I feel no sorority obligation. Nothing.

Ever.

Her voice is fairy—like a comedian's parody of an immigrant in a sitcom, all squeaky like a mouse, her nose twitching as she speaks. "The pipes burst. Just today."

"I can't hear you, sorry." I lean in on her. "What did you mean?"

The only native speaker stays silent. Just when we could do with more information. I look at him: a trapper, lean, tall, underfed, ghostly, fading away back into the past where he belongs. We all have blue eyes in this part of the world. We are amongst Slavs, but none of us belongs to that tribe.

Daan is still playing with his phone. Do something. Do fucking something.

"Daan, are you with us? We need to get the kids to bed. We need a room if theirs has been double-booked. "

Please, make a decision for me. Just this once.

He shrugs. "I'm trying to cancel the reservation."

"Very useful," I answer back.

"Mammie," says Luuk desperately. I do not take his hand. "Paatje," he cries, turning. Daan smiles at him and takes him under his arm. Fucker. Always there for him. What about me? What about us?

"He's okay," I state. "Put him down and make a decision."

"I can't cancel it. I have no network." Daan shows the hosts his phone to prove his point. Why would he be lying?

"I can cancel for you," says Brad. "We have another place up in the hills near the wellness centre. No need to book."

What wellness centre? There was nothing on the web about that. Probably just a stand-in sauna and a paddling pool. I had an English boyfriend at Uni when I was on an Erasmus who laughed at the word. Said it made no fucking sense. There was *health* but no *wellness* in the language. I told him it made sense to the rest of the world. He ought to stop thinking of it as his language now, it belonged to the world. We argued. I went back to the Netherlands and he went silent at the same time. I wrote emails. He never answered. Had I stayed or he had come with me, had we stayed in contact, would I have had children? Would I be me? I feel guilty for the thought. I look at Daan. At Luuk. At the quiet cot.

"The room's been cancelled," says Ebba meekly, phone in hand. Why did we need to cancel? Why not keep the same booking and just change rooms? "You can just pay in cash now, can't you?"

Can we? What's going on? "Daan?" I rupture his stillness.

Daan looks at me. Evi is crying again. Luuk is staring at me. Why me? Who made me the fucking centre of the world?

"You decide," I tell him. He murmurs something no one understands. "Look, fuck,"—Ebba is shocked by my profanity, Daan shrugs again and Brad half-smiles—"it's really late, we've been in the car for days, let's have a look at the place at least."

"My master!" Daan mocks. I want to punch him. "She's a schoolteacher. History. She likes using that tone," he tells

Brad. The American snorts. Ebba looks at me.

I turn to my children. Why did I choose to surround myself with kids? At work, at home. I hate their smell, their noise. Daan. He made me. *He* wanted them. I am what he wants, always what he wants. To keep the peace. My internal walls shiver. The worry descends. I begin to ask Daan whether he is sure.

"Right, that's decided." Daan claps his hands together. What does the clapping add? Yeah, decided. *I* decided again. I watch him walk to the car, hand in hand with Luuk and Evi's car seat in his other hand. Perfect dad. Head of the family.

"I'll get the pram," I shout.

They do not look back to see if I follow.

Ebba has got into her car, but Brad waits, watching Daan as intently as me.

"Pretty kids," he says quietly.

I don't like the way he says it. "Daan!"

III

THE PLACE IS HALF an hour away. I say nothing in the car. I don't even think. My ovaries do all my internal monologuing for me. Evi cries. Luuk asks questions and screams. He rhythmically kicks the back of my seat. I feel his toes puncture through to my insides.

Daan waits impatiently for me to talk. I am silent. I tried telling him I didn't like Brad. He dismissed me, saying *we won't see much of them* and that he was all right, just an American in Europe. *They're all like that*, he tries to reassure.

It's pitch black as we pull up. The headlights illuminate shy phantasms in the trees and old wrinkled faces in their gnarled trunks. We have driven up a single track and suddenly the world falls away. Daan slams on the brakes and Luuk squeals. I sit up and look.

Nothing.

Brad's face at the window, old and gnarled like the bark. "Apologies. Forget to warn you about that."

I get out and stand by Daan. The valley is directly below us, cruelly sliced away from the granite. The two wheels of the car are half a metre from the edge. I feel vertigo, a dizzy heaviness in my legs and blood rushing away from my brain. I imagine myself jumping. Jumping away from Daan's cheeriness, Luuk's screaming fits, Evi's crying—after all, they don't need me. Brad grabs me when I stumble; his hands are strong and a little too friendly. I push myself away,

"Thank you," I say accusingly.

"Ooh, that was close," Daan says next to me. He does not sound concerned.

Not close enough. I take a step forward but am interrupted by Brad's voice. "There it is!" A blinding security light makes me stumble in the other direction.

I hold my side, rubbing it. Dann looks at me. "Are you okay?" He touches me there, on my ovary. He wants to be tender, he always wants to be tender, but he pushes and hurts me. I yelp. His mouth opens to ask me—no, probably to tell me I'm too sensitive. *Too sensitive.* I'm panicking. My ovaries kick harder. It needs to remain a secret. Daan would raise the subject of another child. And I would have to cry. And sob. And acquiesce as he wore me down.

I am saved by Brad. "Come in, come in."

Daan has Evi over his shoulder and Luuk's hand in his. They enter the door, and I follow them in and look around. Bathroom is clean. Beds and sheets are clean. Kitchen is clean.

"It's okay, isn't it?" Daan asks nervously.

I check my phone. There is still no signal to look for hotels online, and when I think of taking that road back down in the dark...

"Yes, it's okay," I sigh.

I lug the suitcase into our room, which is sparse. A few masks on the wall, probably from Thailand. The kids' room is next to ours. There's space for a cot in with us, but Daan will insist Evi sleep with Luuk. Luuk will cry until we let him come with us, and I will end up with her. When Daan has finished with me. At least I will not be alone.

"I'll leave you to it," calls Brad. A car door slams outside. He has gone.

I open the suitcase on the bed. On top is the vibrator. Pink, hard, angry. Daan must have packed it after I had finished the case. It lies offensively on my clothes. Waiting to be used on me. Waiting to make me its object. I imagine Daan watching me as he likes to do. I close the suitcase and leave it unpacked.

IV

We have sex. It is unsatisfying. Daan would call it making love. He pushes and pulls, turns me this way and that. I feel little, let alone love. My friends describe him as sensitive. As thoughtful. I wanted it rough. His aggression at least sees *me*. He is rough when he drinks. When my friends cannot see. I smile at him as he pulls out, giving up and lying on his side. I think about asking him if he minds. I don't know why I should. *I* mind.

My eyes are wet. At least Evi is sleeping.

I pull the sheet tight around me. I imagine being beaten. He kisses my shoulder.

V

Luuk screams. It's dark. I'm up, smashing into cold brick. The small space between the bed and the wall is barely enough to squeeze through. The light is on in the bathroom.

"Help," crashes the word into our room, a high pitched, animalistic sob.

Daan is slowly rising. Sitting up. Calm.

Luuk runs past me, pushing me out of the way, and jumps into the bed. Daan wraps him up in thick arms and murmurs to him. "In there!" Luuk points.

I go into the bathroom to look out of the window and catch a shadow, a dark patch in the black between the trees. It moves, it goes.

"On the floor," Luuk says.

There is a spider. Black and hairy. Heavy and squat. It sits in the centre of the floor of the bathroom, staring at me. Its pedipalps ritualistically clean its face in slow motion. It moves forward two steps.

"Daan!" I shout.

He calls back, "I have the kids. Put it out, don't hurt it." The sort of thing he says in front of others. To convince them he is calm and in control. A friend to all. "You can do it," he adds.

Evi begins to cry, to call out for attention.

I pick up Luuk's abandoned trainer and smash it down hard. The floor has a red and black stain on it. The noise was a crunch.

DAY TWO

VI

IN THE MORNING, I pop the pill and my receptors tingle. A piano concerto in my forehead, soothing away the guilt as I stare at Evi in the pop-up cradle and wonder who she is and where she came from. Luuk is making grating car noises with his cereal spoon at the breakfast table.

Daan rises. "Come on Luuk, let's get going."

"Where are you going?" My voice is shrill, panicky. My eyes are fixed on Evi. She gurgles and smiles. I wait for the crying.

Daan hesitates. "We're going to explore. There's a rope bridge over the stream. Luuk wants to walk it. Tomorrow, we should go for a hike. The forests look great around here."

I sigh. It's involuntary, but he takes it as an offence. He becomes rigid. His hands crunch. I feel crumbs beneath my bare feet and a dread as my eyes fix Evi.

Luuk is up. His spoon is flying and now shooting lasers. At me? At me and not his father. "Come on, Paatje, we've got pirates to fight."

"It's fresh water, not the ocean," I state bitterly, as though the statement even made sense.

"C'mon, Blackbeard," Daan laughs, saving us from the awkward silence.

Luuk stops in front of me. "Did you kill the spider like Mr. Brad killed his dog?"

Daan feels the need to explain. "We were playing when you were sleeping this morning. Brad was outside and told this weird story about how he had to kill a dog because it got rabies."

"Why would he tell Luuk something like that?"

"Yes, why?" asks Luuk, horrified, not understanding my question. "Why did he kill a dog? I like dogs."

I add to Daan's discomfort. "Yeah, why didn't he keep it in a cage or just put it outside?"

He knows I'm talking about the spider, about how I had to be the one to kill it so Luuk would hate me and not him. I prod a bit more. "If I became a rabid zombie, do you think Daddy would keep me in a cage and feed me other people's brains, hey Luuk?"

"C'mon Luuk." Daan pushes him through the door. He stabs me with a glare as he exits. "You'll scare him."

And they're gone. I'm left alone with Evi. She gurgles and I flinch. I sit frozen and immobile, waiting for some instruction about what to do and how to love her. It should be natural, shouldn't it?

VII

HE STAYED. I WAS being polite when Daan finished in the shower and he and Brad were having beer on the terrace. Luuk was with them, pretending his juice was a beer. Brad was explaining how he had ended up in Serbia after his third divorce and Old Europe, outside the EU, allowed him to be more innovative in the wellness sector. To use machinery that was difficult to get and harder to register in the States. There, in the US, medicine was all big business, and they controlled the therapies for profit. In the EU, it was all mafia and pharmaceuticals.

As he spoke, I thought of those broken, bruised women left behind after each divorce, who probably fell from exhaustion into another man's fist.

"Stay for dinner," I said when Daan looked at me. I expected Brad to say no. He'd been talking nonstop about diet, nutrition, what one should eat, how certain vegetables were bad for you. He talks a lot. We were planning to have fish fingers in bread.

"I'll ask Ebba," he said, rolling out of the chair, and now he is back. Alone. He takes another beer. I wonder what it does to his insides, how he balances the rot, the deep intestinal fermentation with his aim to live forever. He told us explicitly he can live forever, that the body only dies if treated badly.

"Ebba?" I ask.

"She doesn't feel well."

I know why, I accuse him internally. *I know why.*

"Blood transfusion," he tells us, "Taking the blood out, filtering it and pumping it back in. Mix it with ozone." He chews on the fish finger sandwich greedily. He gulps the beer. "Eat properly, only pure red meat. Nuts, but not cashews." Random advice. Sounds like the worst treatises from the Middle Ages. He tells us about the expert German doctor he knows. A real doctor. He threatens us with the book.

Daan is diplomatic, but then Brad says an odd thing, "Ideally, young blood is best. One must keep one's blood young. The German advises proper transfusions."

"You don't do that!" I shriek, thinking of the wellness centre which squats in the woods nearby. "Not here."

"No," he responds, "Not blood. We do ozone. We have ozone infusion units. It could do you good."

Ozone? Isn't that in the atmosphere?

"We pump it directly into your veins. Do you know what colour ozone is?" he asks Luuk. Luuk looks at his feet. He is uncomfortable. I expect Daan to help, but he is silent and waiting.

"What colour?" he asks again aggressively.

"Blue," guesses Luuk, more out of fear than volition.

Brad looks disappointed. He does not let us know whether Luuk is correct. This narks me. What fucking colour is ozone? The question has become important.

"Blue?" I ask.

He does not tell me whether I am right. He still looks disappointed, so I believe we got it right. He simply says, "You can live thirty years more."

I don't want to live more.

He goes on; the beer is making him chatty, and Daan always lets others speak. I begin putting Luuk to bed. He resents it. He thrashes, runs when I turn around and screams hysterically. On the terrace, I hear Brad telling Daan how he had been bitten by a spider. His foot had swelled like a football. And, being American, the Serbian hospitals won't look at him. He got Ebba to inject ozone directly into the bite. The day after, he could run ten miles.

I think of the spider, heavy and squat. I think of the spider, crushed and dead.

VIII

"He's full of shit. Ozone? Ozone in the body. Perhaps he is to blame for the hole."

"We don't know everything," placates Daan as we both undress. "He's interesting."

"Next, you'll be telling me to use crystals on Evi's rash."

"Don't be facetious, you get so snappy. Enjoy the break. Relax."

I hate him when he tells me to relax. What he really means is *stop being a bitch*. I continue ranting. "Did you see his skin? It was pale. Stretched thin like parchment."

Daan has been drinking, so he's less indifferent to my prodding. "You get bitchy. You were snappy with him. He's fine."

"I don't trust him. Did you see how he looked at the children?"

"You're paranoid. Not every man is your stepfather."

The comment is directed and deliberate. As accurate as one of his jabs to my ribs. Smiling to guests, joking with friends, and pulling me by my hair when I can't smile when he thinks I should.

"Or you," I prod mercilessly, hoping for him to be rough, but flinching as he turns on me. He looms over me, his face drawn and his eyes raging. He has the vibrator in his hand. He discards it on the bed.

People break people. He goes to the living space, opens his laptop, and the flickers explode on to his lenses. He leans back, his mouth tenses. I know what he's watching; I can hear the grunts and pants. What he wants to copy.

I wash a sleeping pill down with the last of the wine to kill the thoughts.

DAY THREE

IX

DAAN IS SPRAYING OIL on his bike. He had bought a mountain bike. A mountain bike to keep with us back in the Netherlands! He is wasteful with money. His pretence that the break was for me and him to get away, to rupture the routine, to come out of lockdown into not *thesameoldsameold*, is crumbling. I look for Luuk, but Daan is garbed in Lycra, so it is a serious ride. His body is a little too round now to pull it off, as though he'd been the one carrying Evi for nine months.

Looking at the velvet forests infecting the cheeks of the hills, the black-green crawling serpentine away from us, ambling away like a defeated army. *Daan twisting on a gnarled root, the bike flinging him and leaving him in a crooked, bloodied, and broken heap. Food for the forest.*

"Not taking Luuk?" I ask, finger in an open wound. The door to the kitchen is ajar. I hear the drip of the tap. Drip. Drip. Drip. A slow metallic thud as it hits the sink. "He can ride on the back or run along with you," I say when he doesn't answer.

He looks up, some odd tool in his hand that looks like a device for extracting confessions from witches. "Not today. I was hoping for me time."

I bite down on my lip. Drip. Drip. I look at the open door. He follows my gaze. There is a small whimper from the cot. Evi is stirring. Luuk is still eating breakfast. Shovelling the cereal into his mouth, but listening with half an ear. He is hurrying, hopeful still to go with his dad.

I look back at Daan, who is continuing his "me time" by checking every nut on the frame. "I think he wants to go. It'll let me pay attention to Evi."

"He always wants to do things with me." Daan says that deliberately, "I know he does and when he's bigger, he can come. Today, though, it would be good for me to go a bit further. Can you distract him?"

My hand around Luuk's throat, pinning him to a wall. Distracting him. Holding him there as he cries about letting him go. Our eyes raging against one another. Evi screaming from her cot in the other room. His dad cycling along pretty paths. I shake the image from my head.

"I'm not sure that's fair," I say. "This is supposed to be my holiday as well."

Daan picks up a larger tool. He rises to his feet and turns to me. It is then his eyes bind mine. After the lethargic, menacing movement, he holds the tool, all angles and points, up a little. "Not fair? I work really hard at home."

Drip. Drip.

"But," I say, my tone dialling down the prodding, seeing the point of explosion on the horizon and feeling my bruised ribs.

He continues. "Here, I can just go, no pressure, no stress." And then it comes: "You get a lot of free time at home."

Drip. Free time? Change nappy. Drip. Play finger-painting. Drip. Prepare bottle. Drip. Prepare lunch. Drip. Get Luuk to swimming. Drip. Shake Evi as she cries. Drip. And sit alone. Drip. Stare into space. Drip. Cry quietly. Drip.

He adds, almost cruelly, waving the spanner in my face, "Be fair!"

"Fair?"

"Yes," he sighs, his hand in my face. "Be fair."

"Fair? Fucking fair." Drip. "I'm trapped at home with two aliens, doing their every single bidding," drip, "cleaning, cooking, waiting for you," drip, "listening to your shit when you get home and how fucking tired you are," drip. "*Fair*? You, you, who trapped me with these appendages, gave them to me as some supposed gift," drip, "and then just left them and me to stare wordlessly at each other day after day," drip, "then, I have to put your cock in my mouth and like it," drip. "*Fuck your fair!*"

He starts forward. Abrupt. A clumsy movement. *His hand around my throat. Like that one time. After the party when his secretary sprawled herself over him and I pushed him away when we got home. That one time when he let go but didn't want to.* I could see it in his eyes. Like now. The fury rising. Pleasure. The spanner is near my nose. I expect it to flash across my face. To bruise me, to break me, to show on the outside how I am on the inside.

"Tomorrow," he smiles as he backs up. "Tomorrow, I'll take the kids, you can use the spa on the hill."

Do I even want to use a spa? Does he care? I'm trembling. I say nothing. Luuk has put his spoon down, his alien eyes glaring at me as though it's my fault. Pleading to let him go with his father as though I have made the decision.

Daan gets on his bike and is gone.

"Can someone close that fucking tap?" I sob to no one.

X

THE CRYING STARTED AT eleven and didn't stop. Daan was still away on his bike, and Luuk was fighting dragons with a spoon outside the flat.

I could cradle her, hug her, but I didn't. My body remained frozen in the chair, staring at her.

I prepared the milk. She drank.

I prepared a gin and tonic. I drank.

I cried.

Evi cried.

We cried. And could not stop.

I walk out and light a cigarette. Inhale deeply. So deeply. Daan has begun noticing the smell. He knows I'm smoking again. But, always just little hints, nudges, never a direct accusation. If he catches me, it will be more. I become ever more obvious; I blow the smoke on my clothes directly.

Evi is crying inside, so I inhale deeper, louder, vainly.

I should hold her.

I light another cigarette.

Blanket forest spreads before me. Horror of the oppressive green crashes over me. We are truly nowhere.

And the silence.

Evi's silence.

She must be dead. It's my fault. I don't love her.

I am inside.

Brad has Evi in his stringy, naked arms. He's making faces and she's giggling. He is so natural with her. A natural born grandfather. She smiles and gurgles cheerfully. I feel nauseous.

"What the fuck!" I exclaim. "Put her down."

"Daan told me to keep my ears open," says Brad. "Just in case you needed help."

"Ah," I respond, meaning *fucker*. Fucker Daan. Fucker Brad.

"She's a darling. So plump." He lifts her up to take a better look. "A good colour. Usually means healthy blood."

English is his native language, so I wonder whether what he said was not strange in his brain. I reach out and take Evi from him. She sits awkwardly in my arms, her smile disappears and she looks around for anyone else. We reach a compromise and remain silent with one another and the world.

"Have you explored the grounds yet?" Brad asks. "You must see our wellness centre up the hill."

Wellness? I'm starting to agree with my disappeared friend: what an odd word. A worrying word. As though we are all unhealthy, already fallen and in need of machines to heal us, just as religion and prayer were there to heal us once. I think of the witches, the young girls and angry women burned at the stakes, whose history I had corrupted in my dissertation into men's history, to the talk of mass hysteria, of an ideology of social power and discourse, just to be a teacher in a man's world. As I wrote, I could feel the truth under the words. I think of their bodies burning and I knew, I *know*, at the root of it all, it was just because it gave men like Brad a hard-on to watch them burn, to vent their spite when they said no to his cock between their legs. I think of Daan watching me masturbate. I think of men watching. Smiling. I think of the laptop.

"Are you okay?" Brad asks. "Do you want Ebba and me to look after the baby?"

He mentions Ebba casually. All men drop in their appendages to reassure us. My stepfather always began sentences with, *"Your mother and I think..."*

I hold Evi tightly, her cries become shrill. I put her in the crib and she sleeps.

"No, no, I'm fine, thank you."

He does not go. He looks at his flat.

"Well," he says, not looking at me, "if you need me."

He goes. Through the door and gone.

XI

"Just relaxing?"

Fuck, I hate that word.

It's Ebba. She has a sheep with her. It follows her everywhere like a dog. It is old, wool falling from it, and has only one eye. It disgusts me.

"An old member of the family," she tells me. "Won't be with us much longer."

"No?" I innocently reply. "Have you not injected it with ozone?"

She does not smile. Her face is written in wrinkles, hiding bruises. "Brad mentioned you wanted to see the wellness centre. He said you could do with a break." She pauses as we reflect on yet another man knowing what is best for us. "I can take you now, he's having a treatment."

"I'm not sure." I am polite.

Luuk is by me. "I want to go, I want to go, I want to see it," his voice higher with every word until he is screaming.

"Not now Luuk, not now darling," I say.

"Pleaaaassssee..."

"No."

He throws himself on the floor, fists pumping into the ground, tears watering the earth. I drag him up and begin waving a finger in his face. He backs off, sullen.

Ebba takes his hand. "Come," she says, looking harshly at me. "*Come*," she then says to me. I walk into the flat, scoop up a sleeping Evi who looks at me resentfully, and go. I have to now. To show I care.

To show others I care. To do what they say I should.

XII

Luuk is still with Ebba. She talks to him like a kindly grandmother, half bent, whispering. Evi stares at the bright lights, struggling a little in my arms. The wellness centre is an old barn with neon lights and, in the first room, a jacuzzi and small sauna. Bright beanbag chairs slouch embarrassingly around, incongruous and anachronistic.

Brad is dressed in a hospital gown, off-white, ready to share his inner sanctum. He stands too close to me. His open palm rests on the small of my back—in the small of my back, uncomfortably remaining there. His smile is inauthentic, his words are not to be trusted.

"This is the wellness centre," says Ebba, snapping the lights on. As the fluorescent tube flickers for stretched out seconds, machines scrape out of the shadows. Mechanisms of torture against a background of stone walls, low wooden ceilings and a farmhouse floor. Iron maidens, racks, Judas cradles and pearls of anguish. All the images and descriptions of my studies come back to me. The modern technology, a mere veneer for the machines below, the heavy wills of malicious men who would tie you down, touch you and condemn you if you liked it, condemn you if you didn't.

The light steadies itself and the room mocks me. The second room is more clinical and less rustic than the first; sterile, white walls, no windows. Humming medical machines. Neatly stacked, connected to oscillators, screens, and trolley beds. Clean, white sheets.

Brad pushes by me, just too close. "Here we are."

The walls are heavy with condensation but no blood. The smell is bleach and alcohol. Antibacterial fresh, not naturally fresh. No smell of flesh or bodies. I glance at Ebba, her eyes downcast as always, and wonder whether she has been scrubbing, washing away the sins.

Brad begins the tour. He points to machines and explains. The large upright human-sized tube is the athletic heat treatment, the sweat room, and he holds up a vacuum tube to explain the delivery of ozone, showing me various nozzles for the different orifices and a needle. A large needle which would make a hole in a child's skin, big enough to bleed out. He explains it is for "direct delivery".

To my left sits a large pump and two beds. *Blood transfusions. Ebba as Igor, keeping Brad young as children's blood flows into him. I imagine the good, healthy blood of my children in those tubes.* I hold Evi tightly and look round for Luuk.

Brad climbs onto the bed. He deliberately lets his gown open in my line of sight. Ebba says nothing. She hands Luuk to me. His hand is clammy in mine. He tries to free it, but I keep a firm hold.

Brad is going to show us a treatment. Ebba forces the plastic tube into his mouth and it seems to emerge from his anus, spit roasted by a pump. I check Luuk is looking away. Red-blue liquid flows through it and he gurgles helplessly, his medical slip falling apart to show me his testicles, small and shrivelled, between his legs. Ebba pulls levers and throws switches; each time, Brad gags like a porn actress giving head, pretending it is pleasure when all he wants to do is vomit. A huge valve, a robot lung, ascends and descends ever faster, pumping, making his body rise and fall like a slave on a conveyor belt. He reminds me of my wiry stepfather, standing silently by at night while I pretended to sleep.

I imagine the witches. Waterboarded, scalded, pricked, skinned. I see what he is doing as a choice. I see it as a consequence of the videos I've caught Daan watching. I know they want to do it to me. Witches strapped to new versions of old machines, pulling on us, stretching us, reshaping us to be what they want. I look at Ebba's face.

She turns a dial gleefully.

"We must go," I state and turn.

Daan is at the door, his Lycra damp with sweat. He is not horrified. He's curious.

"Let's go," I tell him. He does not move.

Luuk yanks free and runs to him. We walk down the path and he takes Evi from me. She falls asleep in his arms. The machines hum behind us.

"These people are weird," I tell him. "I'm worried for the children."

"You always worry," he says without looking at me.

"I want to go. I mean it; I'm seriously worried."

"But," interrupts Luuk, "you promised. A night hike. You promised."

"No," I say.

"The ghosts," he sobs. "You promised to show me the ghosts in the woods."

Daan looks at Luuk and then at me. "We can't leave until tomorrow anyway. I'll take the kids with me on a walk, you look for another place to stay. The laptop connects to their Wi-Fi. Let's eat and relax for now."

He is humouring me. I hear it in his voice.

DAY FOUR

XIII

THE MORNING. I WAKE. I'm already sobbing. Daan pretends to sleep. I wait for her to cry. The weight of the smothering sadness pushes my lungs down. I take the pill. The mist descends.

I rise and mechanically put breakfast on the table. Daan continues his pretence. I wonder why we have driven two thousand miles to do the same thing we do back home. The hot damp of the forest spews out a mist covering the ground. I look into the trees but see nothing. I turn and see up the hill the small barn of the wellness centre, wondering what Brad is up to in there. Whether Ebba is with him. Serving ozone on a silver tray, no doubt.

Evi has made a noise. Daan is already trying to lever her into the papoose. Luuk is ready, impatient. Daan is clumsy and she's getting frustrated. I look at them. He looks back at me, his eyes pleading. I'm silent and she begins to scream, a banshee's wail rising from my ovaries to the ceiling. He struggles with her arm, attempting to thread the tiny fingers into the restricting cloth straps.

"Just leave her," I snap. His relief is palpable. He plops her back into the cot and smiles at Luuk. They grab pastries and run out of the door. They say nothing to me. They do not look at me. I go back and sit on the bed.

Evi is crying. I take a second pill. I let it stroke my temples from inside.

Almost alone.

I look at the door. I look at the sliver of light which separates its base from the floor. No Daan. No Brad. No Ebba. No Luuk. I think of being young. I think of my stepfather.

He would come to the table at 5:33 p.m. precisely. First, his long, angular shadow would unroll menacingly across the bare floorboards and inflate into the plain, wooden chair before his lanky body would be sitting there. An insubstantial mannequin under the oversized suit. An echo of a human soul. His wrist would be turned in, his elbow a perfect arrow to the open curtains, his eyes melting the watch face. Tall even in the chair, he loomed over me and was almost at eye level with my standing mother.

His face was drawn, skin so tight it was fused to the bone. I used to snatch glances at it when I was sure he would not catch me. It was a parchment-thin canvas stretched across a weak frame, pulled to a point by the angular, sharp nose. I would imagine going to the side of him, to see whether he had any depth at all, but I was too disciplined to move. His washed-out eyes seemed to be ringed by mascara and his glasses were reminiscent of times gone. No facial hair, no rumour he could even grow any, and an Adam's apple that, though as prominent as a rock on the beach, was as motionless as his lips. The tight, cruel lips, starved of blood and joy.

The dinners were without sauces or spices. He could not abide flavour. Just potatoes and broccoli left so long in the water they had become grey.

My mother would always put the first plate in front of him. Without fail. He would wait for all the plates to be on the table, all the time inspecting his watch, and we would wait for him to place his first small, immaculately cut piece of food into his slightly opened mouth before beginning. I was transfixed by the precision of his movements. The perfect cuts with the knife, the protractor-perfect inclination of the cutlery and the head which never moved, seemingly lacking vertebrae. The fact he never apparently chewed or swallowed. I half expected a forked tongue to shoot out and take in the peas one by one.

His eyes remained fixed on what he was doing. He would only raise his arm to look once more at his watch.

The way his suit did not crease reminded me of an insect's carapace. I had never seen him in anything else. Even as he sat on my bed at night. His ties were camouflaged in beige, not daring to invite attention.

I kept my eyes downcast. In the early days, my mother had tried to ask questions about the numbers he checked at work, about the tax and the profits, but his monosyllabic and disdainful answers were offered only because he had to while being aware she asked only because she thought she had to. Soon even their voices were replaced by the loud ticking of the mantle clock, joining my own lost words.

And the sighs of disapproval when we chewed too loudly.

We could never finish our plates before him, our masticating timed to the regular checks he made of the functional watch on his wrist. And we could not finish too long after him. His stare would take the knife and fork from our hands and force them down onto the plate. An arranged marriage of two metal corpses, laid together at six o'clock, even if we had not finished our meal.

And he would unroll to his full height, the room shrinking about us. A ledger of bones held together by the pinstripes of his suit, the hair on his head a mockery of the present. As he turned and walked away, his shadow would remain for a few seconds longer than the light should allow.

It was the same shadow I would see at 9:38 p.m., sneaking purposively under my door to steal breath from my lungs and beats from my heart as I used the duvet as some sort of pathetic ward.

I think of Ebba. I think of Evi. I think of Brad.

My anxiety is high. I need to sleep. I put myself into bed, checking the cot and hoping Daan and Luuk hurry back. When I wake, I shall start packing and we will leave.

There is a shadow creeping under the threshold of the door. I curl up into the duvet and let sleep take me. I am not sure how many pills I've taken.

XIV

I INHALE THE SMOKE on the patio. The forest is angry. It has swallowed my family. It's dark and they have not returned. No sound, no Luuk nor Daan. Evi still sleeps. Or did she go with Daan? I'm confused for a moment, the mix of antidepressants, wine, and sleeping pills stroking my forehead like a fog.

We need to book somewhere else. Inside, I stare at the clothes, the empty suitcases, my lethargy laid out before me. Daan and Luuk should be back by now. My phone still has no signal. I vainly hold it higher, not sure why. I pour a little more wine and drop a pill on my tongue. That is enough for today. I remember Daan's anger, the blows, the last time I slipped into a stupor.

We need a place to stay. A hotel. From the laptop I can send a message as well, an email if it connects to the Wi-Fi as Daan says. The laptop's ghostly light throws menacing shadows on the wall.

And there they are. The videos left provocatively open

for me to see. Women tied to walls, in masks, bent over desks. Women stretched this way and that, hair pulled, eyes wide, mouths gagging. To the world, he is perfect. A perfect husband. A perfect father. Like my stepfather was perfect. They never see them late at night, a bad day at work, whisky in hand. Sorry for what they've done. They never see them sobbing at the end of the bed, asking forgiveness, knowing full well they will do it again. Men can be perfect, the world allows them. Women are flawed. We are all flawed. Fallen victims through all the fault of our own.

I shut. It is late.

Evi is still quiet. Too quiet. Her cot has been silent all afternoon.

I pour a bit more wine into my glass. When did I last check on her? What have I done all day? My mind resists my attempts to open it. I walk to the cot and peer over.

The remembered hands of my stepfather reach deep into my lungs and tear the air out. Daan's fists pound my stomach to bend me over. Brad holds my head down and my mouth is silently agape.

Where is she?

I look again. Under the cot, under the bed, a sob escapes from my throat in the shape of her name.

I rush room to room followed by the ghosts of violent

men. Nowhere. She is nowhere. Nowhere am I alone.

In the bathroom, a small puddle of blood blackens in the centre where I had smashed the spider. The wellness centre with its tubes, its machines, its horrors painfully sear my mind.

"Are you okay?"

I turn violently and grab Ebba by the shoulders. I push her to the wall. A guttural roar, "Evi!"

She shies back, squirming from my feeble press. I look away, ashamed. "I'm sorry." Bewilderment momentarily steals my rage. "But do you have Evi? She has gone. Evi has gone, and Daan," my rage rising again, "did not come back today with Luuk."

"Is the car still there?" asks Ebba and although she has the voice of a fairy, that is a fucker of a question, one which penetrates under my skin and scrapes at my insides. "I thought I heard the doors open earlier."

I run to the window. "Yes," I answer her. "Yes."

"I'm sure he must have come and taken Evi. Have you tried calling?"

The puddle of blood in the bathroom comes to my mind. "Where's Brad?"

She ignores my question but passes me her phone. "I know you have little or no signal, use my phone."

I look at the screen, unsure of what to do. I don't know

my husband's number. Who knows numbers anymore? I grab mine from the desk and open his contact. I clumsily type the number, twice almost dropping my phone.

Ringing. A painful, banal melody. Neither happy nor sad. His phone hums in the bedroom where he must have left it. But he never does. I look at Ebba. She does not seem surprised.

"Where's Brad?" I ask again.

"I left him having a treatment."

Brad on the table, a tube from his mouth drinking the blood of my children, strapped fast in nearby chairs. Ebba is still impeccable. Daan, bound and bleeding in a locked room. A failure of a father, unable to protect his offspring. Ebba does not move.

In a flash, I strike her around the head with her own phone. She stumbles, blood trickling down the centre of her forehead, rising and falling with the pronounced wrinkles. I strike her again; this time her skull hits the wall.

I drag her unconscious body into the bedroom. She weighs nothing, there is nothing substantial about her. There is Daan's phone. One missed call. A smutty text from his secretary. The suitcase has been packed. It's obvious Brad and Ebba were going to drive off and say we never left or never arrived. I try to shake the drowsiness. They must have drugged me. Perhaps Daan too.

I tie Ebba's hands behind her back with a pair of my tights. I put a pair of knickers in her mouth and wrap another pair of tights around her head to hold them in place. I push her into the centre of the bed.

With her phone I type in my mum's number back home, once again copying it clumsily from my phone. I walk into the kitchen and while the phone rings, I take a knife from the kitchen drawer and slip it into the belt of my trousers. The phone rings off, I push redial.

There is a knock at the door. Daan? I throw it open, expectant.

XV

"Have you seen Ebba?" Brad is still in his gown. Just as I was about to search for him, I open the door to find him before me. No Luuk. No Daan. No Evi. "She was supposed to come back." His eyes flare anger. His body angles itself over me like Nosferatu's shadow.

Keeping my eyes locked on his, I feel her phone, hidden behind my back, aggressively shrug each time my shaking, nervous finger hits a letter. It's like a petulant teenager pushing back; so often the centre of attention, the phone is being used in a distracted way and it does not like it.

We sit at the table. I have to listen to his words, feign interest, don't let my mind wander. His anger has subsided and he has fallen into his normal monologues about health. I chide myself and smile at him. Natural, I tell myself, keep it natural as my finger moves secretly under the table, sliding rhythmically, falling into line with his syllables. Tap, tap. It's easy: his American accent is flat, evenly spaced, devoid of life.

Yet, *yet*, still threatening.

I nod and grunt, hoping it's in time, hoping it is not out of place. My finger moves upward, top left where the blue arrow should be. I realise how I am so dependent on my eyes, but they are chained to his, imprisoned by his monologue about oxygen in the blood and poor digestion of vegetables. About the treatment he was having. I continue to nod.

I inwardly jump at a longer shake, as though the phone has just emerged growling and buoyant from a river. Ready to play again. I keep my outward, passive state. He suspects nothing.

I begin to type the message again. Two simple words. Over and over again. I have no idea what my clumsy, blind fingers and the malicious auto-text are concocting. My intention is simple: "help" and "Mila".

I want to tell my mother everything. Where we are. The danger. What happened at night in her house. That, though, is all beyond the dexterity of my sightless fingers.

He is still talking. Oblivious to the fate of his wife. Indifferent to my children bound in his dungeon, my husband bleeding out on a floor somewhere. He whitters on, "Corn and beans. They get stuck in your gut, you can't pass them through and they break the intestine wall. Makes a terrible mess."

"Aha," I play it neutral. Not sure if I should go full-interested or cautiously agree because it is obvious.

He stops and looks at the bedroom door. He has heard the thud. The hollow bang.

I say nothing.

I slip the phone into my jeans' pocket. It will bulge, he will probably see it. My hand passes over to the hilt of the knife. Also visible, no doubt. I thrust my breasts up to distract him.

"Do you want tea? Let me get some biscuits," I tell him and rise, "They're still in the suitcase. All the way from Rotterdam."

He's been going on about healthy foods and I'm offering him butter and sugar. He didn't say no. Hypocrite. When he's not looking, I open the door and enter.

Ebba's eyes are terrified. She has been banging her bound feet on the headboard. She gasps and the gag goes into her mouth, making her choke. I bang the lid of the suitcase loudly and shush her with an angry gesture.

I see some tears. Little beads of water running down her cheek. I can see she has been struggling to free herself. The sheet has rucked up around her. She winds her feet back up to bang once more.

I take the first object to hand out of the suitcase and

smack her round the head with it. She sobs quietly. It is my vibrator. It turns on and starts humming.

I mouth, *Silence.*

From the other room: "Y'know, I'm surprised Ebba didn't come here. She said she had heard a few bangs."

"I can just re-boil the kettle for more tea if she comes," I call back and fix Ebba once more with my eyes. She curls further into herself.

The phone trembles in my pocket. I snatch it and look. Not my mother. I check the messages I had sent. They make enough sense, but still no reply.

Brad's chair scrapes on the floor.

I strike Ebba again, right in the eye, and am outside with the door closing behind me.

He is looking in the kitchen, opening cupboards. I stand still and watch him. He is tall, no need to raise himself up on his toes to reach the top doors.

He sees me. "Biscuits?"

I am again struck by the disconnect between his ideas, all holier-than-thou eating habits, and his actions. Everything about him is a lie.

"They're here," I say, holding out my hand.

Brad looks at the pink, knobbly shaft in my fist. It's still on, humming like a small drill. Not biscuits at all. I play it smoothly. Turn the vibrator off, nonchalantly put it on the table, and walk to the cupboards. Reach up to take some biscuits we had put away when we arrived.

The phone drops from my pocket, pushed out by my action of stretching upwards. It falls on the floor. His eyes, which I am sure were on my breasts, drop down and see his wife's phone. The damn one-eyed sheep on her lock-screen.

Bang.

And a whimper.

Our attention snaps to the closed bedroom door.

He takes a step toward it.

I stand in front of him. "Must be my suitcase, I left it on the edge of the bed."

Her phone vibrates. The sheep is still there.

Then, the sobs. Loud, despairing sobs. And shuffling. The scraping of flesh over stone tiles.

We both move to the door. He pushes past me and I plunge the knife into his side. He crumples on to the floor. Already a puddle of blood spreads out below him, staining his gown red. I grab the vibrator, turn it on, trying to shove the humming member into the open wound. He screams, so I plunge it into his mouth instead.

"Where are my fucking kids?" I demand. He gags unresponsively. "Daan, where is Daan?"

I yank open the bedroom door. Ebba slumps at my feet.

I place the knife at her throat. "Where are my kids? *Where are they?*"

Brad looks to the door. I look. Nothing.

"Let's go." I kick him in the balls. "Let's go to your wellness centre, let's go now."

XVI

THE BARN DOOR OPENS into the clinic's reception. As we approach the second door, I can hear the machines humming. I hope Evi is still alive. I can't hear her crying. Luuk will be sobbing quietly. "Open it." I push the blade into Ebba's skin, breaking it.

"*Bitch*," Brad spits the word at me. I've heard worse.

He turns on the light. It flickers so brightly it renders me momentarily blind. He grabs something from his left and smashes it against my head. Glass shatters as I stumble to my knees.

Terror grips me as I think of Evi and Luuk. I think of Daan as well. Weak Daan, unable to protect them like me. I remember the small puddle of blood and images crash in on my mind, waves of nauseating stinging liquid polluted with discarded glass slash at my thin, vulnerable skin.

The waves of nausea invite survival. A new me, a raging, she begins to rise. The slashes of discarded glass energise, each cut a reason to act, each slice of skin an angry order.

My hand curls around a metal tube. Big enough to deliver ozone, uncomfortable enough to be forced into a vagina as I imagine Brad's leering face taking pleasure in the suffering necessary for betterment. I smash him round the jaw, the metal penis's shaped tip smacking the back of the head. Blood stains the wheelchair as he slumps into it. Not unconscious but stunned enough for me to tie the straps.

Ebba is frozen in fear. I pick up the knife she has left alone on the floor. For once, she's looking directly into my eyes. Using the tubular dildo as a spear, I send her stumbling back into the heat treatment sarcophagus. I slam the door and turn the heat dial to maximum.

"Wh..." mumbles Brad. I whack him again on the head.

"Do you want me to mummify her?" I scream. Spittle from my rage soaks his face. I'm watching myself from outside, floating above this maternal horror, hiding behind ancestral genetic amorality.

I pump the metal tube into his mouth, making sure he gags. Pounding the back of his throat again and again. Ebba knocks on the glass window weakly, pathetically. Her skin is turning red, beginning to blister. It smells like seared pork.

I lean in close to Brad's face, tube held threateningly under his nose. "Do you care about her? Do you love her like a mother loves her children?"

He opens his mouth to speak, but I don't want to hear his lies, so I plunge the tip once more into his mouth, into his oesophagus. In and out, letting him breathe just enough. Face fucked. Deep-throating. Do you enjoy it, Brad?

"Where is my fucking family?" I scream as I lift his gown, turn on the machine; the blue liquid begins to angrily bubble as I lower the tube between his legs.

"The dose!" he sobbingly begs, coughing vomit.

"Fuck the dose. My children!" I pick up a mallet, one used to test reflexes in knees, but hard like brick. When he only cries, I lean down, whisper in his ear. "*Tell me.*"

XVII

I OPEN THE DOOR to the wellness centre. The outside air is absent of the smell of seared flesh, sweat, fear, and shit. It is pure. I feel my ovary is less swollen; I move more easily.

I push Brad into the open. I still have the reflex mallet in my hand. The wheelchair has a squeaky wheel and rolls like a vandalised shopping trolley. His head lolls to the left, and he mumbles unintelligibly like a child. Most of the blood has dried around his mouth. The bruise on his temple is bright purple with red train-tracks running through it. I think of a journey. From here to…well, just about anywhere. I give him credit where it's due—old, tall Brad, sitting broken and bound in the wheelchair: he kept his secrets.

And those secrets are my family, my children, my life. Buried, no doubt, in the woods that stretch to the mountaintops all around.

I take one of my cigarettes, pop it between my lips and light it. I douse him in the pungent chemicals from the lab. His incoherent grumbling continues. *The young girls through the ages, no doubt belonging to these woods who, because they would not let the old man touch their knees or put his hand up their skirts, were bound to a stack of wood and burned for being dark and evil.* Brad would have done that. I know he would.

I lean into him and play with the fag in my fingers, enticing the orange, crackling embers with my breath. "Last chance. Where are my children?"

Through broken teeth and swollen jaw, he murmurs, "Don't know."

Resilient, our Brad.

"Are you sure?"

"Fuck you," he whimpers. He has tears in his eyes.

Fuck me? No, Brad, fuck you. I look at the smouldering end of the cigarette, the promise of revenge. Justice, almost.

There is a sound from the trees. A creaking branch, a snapping twig. Are those laughing yet whiny voices I hear? I run to the path, leaving behind the broken body of an old man tied to a chair. I wait to see them, to greet them. To hug them. Is that the jaunty sound of my husband's voice, a toddler on his shoulders and a baby in his arms, walking joyfully up the path? Daan and the kids strolling cheerily my way—all mud, dirt, and smiles—before seeing me—all grime, blood, tears, torn, broken. Daan will run to me and I will confess, tell him gently, "I've done it again," and add "I'm sorry." He'll clean up. He'll clean me up. Put the children to bed and tell me everything is going to be all right, make everything go away and make the forgetting possible. He'll tell me it is not my fault. He'll be angry at first, and I'll deserve what I get, but then we'll talk to someone. I'll tell him I do not want to talk. He knows what to do. Just another one of my silly mistakes. We'll put Brad's teeth back in, straighten his fingers, apologise about his dead wife. We'll have a beer together and laugh it all off.

But there is no one. No one emerges from the woods. They aren't coming. There were the woods and the sounds of nature crawling their way to me, disapproving of me.

I turn back to Brad. We are still alone, the two of us. I look at my car. There's a bloodied handprint on the back. I look at Brad.

"You've put them in my car."

He shakes his head.

"Where are my keys? Do you have my keys?"

He shakes his head again.

And then I put my hand into my jeans' pocket and feel the plastic and metal. I take the keys out. They've been there all along. Brad has never touched them. Memories flash like a blade through my brain. *Anger. Rage. Fury.*

Blood.

And no Brad.

I approach the car and place my hand over the print. It is a perfect match. I open the large boot. The bags are still there, one large, one small. Sodden. Smelling. There is a stain on the upholstery. That would anger Daan. He will bring that up one night. Would have brought it up. Now he is silent.

"Sorry," I say. "It's not my fault. A silly mistake."

Evi gurgles. She has been a good girl on her blanket. Quiet as a mouse. I take her in my arms. She does not cry. She begins rooting at my breast.

I push the two black bags aside to make room for another two bodies and glance back at Brad. Then, it comes to me. He is almost dead. He has no spirit left. I cut his bonds and let his body slump to the ground. I pick up a reflex mallet. Envision it being used on my knees to see them jump. And then I smash it into my forehead, holding Evi tight as she laughs at my strange movement. Two, three times, violently, and then sluggishly place the instrument into Brad's hand.

I take his phone. It has a signal. I dial 113 and scream the word, *"Help!"*

David Rose is newly Italian after being an anglo-Scot all his life (but mostly an anglo). He still lives in England. For now, but it is hard. And still teaches philosophy. For now. He publishes mostly horror and fantasy, is currently working on a werewolf novel. He has published a few horror stories here and there, and innumerable pieces on philosophy. An urban gothic novel, *A Day Before Tomorrow, One Day After Yesterday*, resides rather uncomfortably on Amazon.

David on Amazon

Content Warnings

Standard warnings for horror tropes (violence, death, murder) apply to all Graveside Press books.

allusions to postpartum depression and psychosis
mentions of sexual, physical, and emotional abuse
filicide

Thank You!

*Thank you for supporting Graveside Press and our authors.
One of the biggest ways you can help is to leave a star rating
or a review wherever you purchased your copy!*

STAY SPOOKY.

Wanna come hang out with the ghouls?
gravesidepress.carrd.co

Stay up to date with Graveside news and exclusive stories.
graveside-press.com